Stay Up to Date with Sylvia Price

Subscribe to Sylvia's newsletter at http://newsletter.sylviaprice.com[1] to get to know Sylvia and her family. It's also a great way to stay in the loop about new releases, freebies, promos, and more.

As a thank-you, you will receive several FREE exclusive short stories that are not available for purchase.

---

1.   http://newsletter.sylviaprice.com/

HOPE
for Hannah's
LOVE
Amish Love Through the Seasons
SHORT STORY
SYLVIA PRICE

SYLVIA PRICE
EVE
AN ELIJAH COMPANION STORY

Finding Healing (Rainbow Haven Beach Prequel)

Sylvia Price

Published by Sylvia Price, 2023.

This is a work of fiction. Similarities to real people, places, or events are entirely coincidental.

FINDING HEALING (RAINBOW HAVEN BEACH PREQUEL)

First edition. April 17, 2023.

Copyright © 2023 Sylvia Price.

ISBN: 979-8223410317

Written by Sylvia Price.

Table of Contents

Praise for Sylvia Price's Books

"Wow, what a great start to a new series, and I really enjoyed reading it as it was so well-written, and I can't wait to read the next book. This is the first book that I have read by Sylvia Price but not the last and I recommend you read it and you will not be disappointed."

"Author Sylvia Price wrote a storyline that enthralled me. The characters are unique in their own way, which made it more interesting. I highly recommend reading this book. I'll be reading more of Author Sylvia Price's books."

"I love the way this is a very real example of one of the beauties of these small towns! Of course, mixing in beautiful scenery and the growing love with an old friend makes this the perfect start to a new series!"

"I've read several books written by Sylvia Price; she has done a great job at writing a good short story; she is becoming one of my favorite authors. I can't wait to read more of books her books."

"The storyline caught my attention from the very beginning and kept me interested throughout the entire book. I loved the chemistry between the characters."

"The plot flows easily, and the characters are appealing. It's a great story that shows what is most important in life."

"A wonderful, sweet and clean story with strong characters. Now I just need to know what happens next!"

"I just could not put this book down. Thank you for a delightful read."

"I love Sylvia's books because they are filled with love and faith."

"Sylvia's books ooze with love and goodness."

Other Books by Sylvia Price

Songbird Cottage Beginnings (Pleasant Bay Prequel) – FREE
The Songbird Cottage (Pleasant Bay Book 1)
Return to Songbird Cottage (Pleasant Bay Book 2)
Escape to Songbird Cottage (Pleasant Bay Book 3)
Secrets of Songbird Cottage (Pleasant Bay Book 4)
Seasons at Songbird Cottage (Pleasant Bay Book 5)
The Songbird Cottage Boxed Set

The Crystal Crescent Inn (Sambro Lighthouse Book 1)
The Crystal Crescent Inn (Sambro Lighthouse Book 2)
The Crystal Crescent Inn (Sambro Lighthouse Book 3)
The Crystal Crescent Inn (Sambro Lighthouse Book 4)
The Crystal Crescent Inn (Sambro Lighthouse Book 5)
The Crystal Crescent Inn Boxed Set

Sarah (The Amish of Morrissey County Prequel) – FREE
Sadie (The Amish of Morrissey County Book 1)
Bridget (The Amish of Morrissey County Book 2)
Abigail (The Amish of Morrissey County Book 3)
Eliza (The Amish of Morrissey County Book 4)
Dorothy (An Amish of Morrissey County Christmas Romance)

The Amish of Morrissey County Boxed Set

The Origins of Cardinal Hill (The Amish of Cardinal Hill Prequel) – FREE
The Beekeeper's Calendar (The Amish of Cardinal Hill Book 1)
The Soapmaker's Recipe (The Amish of Cardinal Hill Book 2)
The Herbalist's Remedy (The Amish of Cardinal Hill Book 3)
The Amish of Cardinal Hill Complete Series

A Promised Tomorrow (The Yoder Family Saga Prequel) – FREE
Peace for Yesterday (The Yoder Family Saga Book 1)
A Path for Tomorrow (The Yoder Family Saga Book 2)
Faith for the Future (The Yoder Family Saga Book 3)
Patience for the Present (The Yoder Family Saga Book 4)
Return to Yesterday (The Yoder Family Saga Book 5)
The Yoder Family Saga Boxed

The Christmas Cards: An Amish Holiday Romance

The Christmas Arrival: An Amish Holiday Romance

Seeds of Spring Love (Amish Love Through the Seasons Book 1)
Sprouts of Summer Love (Amish Love Through the Seasons Book 2)
Fruits of Fall Love (Amish Love Through the Seasons Book 3)
Waiting for Winter Love (Amish Love Through the Seasons Book 4)
Amish Love Through the Seasons Boxed Set

Jonah's Redemption: Book 1 – FREE
Jonah's Redemption: Book 2
Jonah's Redemption: Book 3
Jonah's Redemption: Book 4
Jonah's Redemption: Book 5
Jonah's Redemption Boxed Set

Elijah: An Amish Story of Crime and Romance

Chapter One

Kenneth Campbell, Beloved Husband and Father, Taken Much too Soon. July 8, 1960—August 24, 2021. Beth Campbell's gaze lingered over the familiar words etched both into the gray marble headstone and her heart.

Biting her lower lip in an effort to control her emotions, Beth ached at the paradox of how it had been almost nine months since she lost her husband, yet it felt like a lifetime in so many ways. Ken was sick for so long, and the cancer had ravaged his body for years before he finally succumbed to the disease and went to meet his Maker in Heaven.

"I miss you, Kenneth," Beth whispered, yielding to the urge to kneel and running her fingertips tenderly over the letters. "I miss you so much that it's crazy. I don't even know who I am without you."

It was the truth. Ken had been her number one fan and main support system for thirty-five years. When she came to the city of Ottawa with little more than a seed of a dream and a plan for the future, Ken had come alongside her and helped her to navigate and learn the ropes of the big city. More than that, he was the one who propped her up when her plans fell apart, and he had been the one to show her that there was more to life than just fame and glory.

"We didn't always have the best life," Beth murmured. "And we might have been tempted to call it quits more than once, but we sure worked our way through all our struggles. How I wish I could hear your voice just one more time."

But she would never hear Ken's voice again. Until she got to Heaven and joined him, that is. A great chasm divided them now that they were literally in different worlds, and the knowledge of it tore at her heart day after day. Swallowing thickly, she shook her head and tried to push aside the gloomy thoughts that constantly plagued her mind, like how she wished she could have joined him in death so they wouldn't have been separated like this.

The surrounding markers and headstones in the large graveyard came into focus as her gaze wandered beyond Ken's grave. Beth considered her life: fifty-eight years old, beyond successful at her job at a popular Canadian women's magazine, a top earner among her peers, and now the inheritor of a highly successful pharmaceutical company that Ken had owned and operated. Her life had always been one that others admired and even envied, but none of that mattered anymore. Regardless of what material possessions she might have or what great accolades she had earned for herself, at the end of the day, Beth felt nothing but a vast emptiness. Her future loomed bleak and miserable, with only the prospect of death something to look forward to.

"Mom?" Her daughter, Lillie, spoke up nearby, alerting Beth that she was no longer alone.

Hurrying to dab away any runny mascara, Beth tried to put on a happy front for her daughter. Lillie had taken her Spring Break to come stay with her mother, and despite Beth's best efforts, it seemed like she couldn't hide her profound sadness from her daughter.

"Mom." Lillie walked toward her mother's side, her brows knitting together in concern.

Today, even her wide blue eyes and fair complexion couldn't draw the attention from the worry lines etched into her face. "Mom, you've been standing out here for almost an hour now. I tried to wait in the car like you asked, but I was starting to get worried."

Faking a cheery smile, Beth shook her head and replied, "I'm so sorry. I guess I just lost track of time. It's been a while since I've been here to see your dad, and I just found it hard to pull myself away."

It was only three days since Beth had last been to the cemetery. But how could she admit the truth to her daughter? That a day without visiting Ken's grave felt like a month. How could she confess to Lillie that more of her heart was in the graveyard with Ken than was beating in her chest?

Heaving a sigh, Lillie nodded and directed her own gaze toward the stone. "Yeah. It's hard to believe he's gone. Sometimes, I still find myself wanting to pick up the phone to call him." Laughing, she added, "Not that he would have time to talk. I'm sure there would be some important business meeting to distract him, but it would be nice to hear his voice."

The words hurt, but they were true. Ken Campbell had been a man devoted to his work above all else. Yet, where did all his slaving get him?

Reaching out to twine her arm around her mother's, Lillie offered a sad tight smile. "I thought that we were going to go out to that little restaurant you like for lunch. I don't know about you, but my stomach is rumbling!" Holding up her black purse as if to prove that she could help take care of any problems, she winked as she added, "My treat! Let's get going before they quit serving lunch."

Beth perused her daughter thoughtfully. Paying for lunch was the least of Beth's concerns. It seemed that money was all she had now—and an abundance of it. Nodding in her daughter's direction, she tried to silence her sad thoughts. "You're right. Let's get going."

Turning her head, she gazed toward the marble stone one last time, allowing the scene to be burned into her memory—something she could recall in her moments of solitude when Ken's absence nearly suffocated her in its oppression, to remind her of her harsh new reality: Ken was gone. It was so hard to leave him behind. It felt like Beth was leaving the best part of her life while she was forced to forge on with the meaningless parts, but, for now, she was going to have to pull her mind away from the overwhelming sadness and focus on at least appearing to be moving forward to Lillie. She wasn't going to let Lillie's Spring Break be a depressing disaster.

Please, God, Beth prayed as she followed her daughter toward the waiting car. *Give me something in life. Give me some reason to keep on going.*

Beth could only hope that the Lord would hear her heart's cry and answer her prayer. She couldn't keep going on this way forever.

SEATED ACROSS FROM her mother in the restaurant, Lillie munched down on a crispy French fry and racked her brain for something to say. She was only two days into her Spring Break, yet it was quickly becoming obvious that her mother was not in a good frame of mind.

Lillie had initially hoped her time away from university would give her a chance to settle her own tumultuous thoughts. She had myriad personal problems of her own to deal with, but it was starting to feel as though her break was focused on nothing but cheering her mom up and trying to drum up upbeat things to say and do. She didn't mind helping her mom through her tough season, but it was keeping her from spending time considering and resolving her own problems, which weren't getting any clearer.

Lillie watched as Beth stared vacantly at her untouched sandwich. Judging by her mother's prominent cheekbones and slightly sunken features, Beth hadn't been eating much lately. Lillie silently scolded herself for not doing more to keep up with her mother and reach out more often since her father's death. She should've been here for her mother, but her attention had been elsewhere. Her father had never made much time for her or her elder brother, so his passing hadn't had the impact it otherwise might have. Instead, her focus had been on her studies at university and...Lukas. She instinctively cut off the thought, stomach churning. *I promised myself not to go there until I'm ready to discuss it with Mom, and I have to stick to that.*

As she watched her mother pick listlessly at the food on her plate, it dawned on Lillie that there wasn't going to be a good time to discuss her boyfriend troubles with her mother for the foreseeable future. Beth was barely holding herself together, a shell of her former self, and she was reliant on Lillie too much for Lillie to even consider Mom helping with her daughter's issues. *I'm going to have to deal with the Lukas situation on my own.*

Swallowing and blinking back the tears prickling her eyes, Lillie forced aside thoughts of Lukas, scooted forward in her seat, and asked, "Have you heard anything from Brian lately?"

She suspected her brother hadn't bothered to spend much time with Beth, whether it be helping with practicalities such as errands or just being with her and giving her the space to talk about things, though he was in the area and checked in now and again to make sure their mother was okay. It was more a question to drag both their minds away from their respective troubles.

Shaking her head, Beth lifted her napkin to dab at her lips; whether it was by reflex or in an attempt to convince Lillie she'd eaten, Lillie wasn't certain.

"No," she murmured. "No, I actually haven't talked to him since Christmas." Almost as if to excuse his behavior, she added, "You know how busy he is."

Six years her senior, Brian was married, with a toddler and a successful law practice. If anyone had a right to claim that he was busy, it was Brian, yet anger percolated in Lillie's belly at the knowledge that he had totally deserted their mother when she needed them most.

"How are things going at the magazine?" Lillie tried to change direction at the palpable sadness on her mother's face at the mention of Brian. "Any new or exciting changes there?"

Raising her shoulders and then lowering them limply, Beth admitted, "Oh, it's about the same as always. I go in each morning and write meaningless drivel that women are anxious to read, and then I go home at night." She met Lillie's gaze with an almost bitter smile as she said, "It's funny that so many women spend their days hanging onto every word about how to look perfect when none of it is going to matter in the end. How many people actually look back on their lives and wish that they had known how to better contour their makeup or pluck their eyebrows perfectly?" Almost as quickly as the words were off her lips, Beth shook her head and hurried to add, "I'm sorry for my attitude, Lillie. You know I'm not usually like this. It's just...well, the last few years have really taken a toll on me. I suppose everything just really feels like it's been put in perspective."

Lillie could remember a time when the magazine had been her mother's biggest passion. She had rushed home many a night and stayed up late working on an article to perfect it in time for publication. To see such a contrast in Beth's attitude both broke Lillie's heart and left her deeply worried about her mother. Glancing from her sandwich back up at her mother's face, Lillie dared to ask the question that was forefront on her mind. "Mom...are you okay? I mean, *really* okay?"

Beth stared back at her with a blank expression and then shook her head. "I don't know," she whispered, answering honestly. "I really don't know. I just wish that there was some way to get away from here...go somewhere for a little vacation to reset myself..."

"Why don't you?" Lillie grabbed onto the first sign of engagement in months that she had observed in her mother. "Be spontaneous—get a ticket for a cruise or something and enjoy yourself."

For a moment, a spark of hope lit in Beth's eyes, but it was quickly snuffed out. Shaking her head, she replied, "No, I don't think so. I'd better not."

Continuing their meal in silence, Lillie prayed that something would happen to change her mother's mind or at least to add a little bit of hope and happiness to her otherwise seemingly dismal existence.

Chapter Two

Pulling up and parking in front of her large two-story townhouse, Beth wished that she had been able to offer a little more cheer in front of her daughter. She had been so determined to hold her attitude together during Lillie's brief week-long Spring Break from university and be good company, yet it was already proving to be impossible. She felt as though stifling her despondency and melancholy were akin to trying to stuff a huge sleeping bag in that ridiculously small sack that comes with it—the more you squeeze one side in, the more the other side pops out and refuses to succumb to being shoved into the sack.

On the short drive home from lunch, Beth noticed Lillie's changed demeanor: she had quit trying to make small talk and stared wordlessly out the window of the vehicle instead. Beth almost wished poor Lillie had gone on Spring Break somewhere else. Surely, her twenty-year-old daughter would have had a more pleasant time enjoying her vacation with her boyfriend, Lukas.

Before either of them exited the car, Beth, gripping the door handle, forced herself to say, "Lillie, I'm so sorry that I'm such a downer. It's just so difficult to move on and derive joy from life again once you lose someone with whom you shared your life for so long." Braving a wavering smile in spite of her grim feelings, she added, "I'll be okay."

Lillie nodded, but Beth could tell that her daughter didn't believe her.

Making her way up the steps to the front door, Beth reached into the mailbox and pulled out a handful of mail. She hardly glanced at it until they were inside the house. Stopping by the table in the large foyer, Beth began to sort through the endless junk mail and notices. Her eyes stopped when she came across an envelope bearing familiar handwriting.

"Maybe tonight we can stay in?" Lillie suggested in the background. "You and I could just have a girls' night where we sit on the couch and watch old movies together... Would you like that?"

But Lillie's words were a million miles away to Beth. Turning the envelope over, she tore into it, pulling out a small card with a picture of a beautiful beach scene on the front. Transported in time, Beth felt like she were a little girl again, standing on those same sandy shores and watching boats in the distance.

Flipping the card open, she silently drank in the message.

"What's that?" Lillie made her way back to her mother's side, shedding her thin jacket and tossing it into a nearby chair. Peering over Beth's shoulder, she tried to read the text.

Clearing her throat, Beth announced huskily, "It's from my childhood friend, Kathy. Do you remember her from the funeral?"

Lillie shook her head.

Of course her daughter wouldn't remember. There were so many people there that it had been hard even for Beth to keep track of them all.

"Kathy sent me a letter. She's written to tell me that she's hoping I might be interested in helping her with a new project. She's renovating and reselling a house with buyers already lined up for the purchase, but she hasn't gotten the interior painted. She says she remembers how I was always a maestro with a paintbrush and hopes I might come stay for a few days and help out. She's promised to reimburse me for my time and to pay for my ticket." Beth smiled a little as she re-read the last line. "And she thinks I could use a change of scenery."

As Beth finished summarizing, hope sparked anew in her heart. Could it be real? Could Kathy have actually sent her this message the very day that Beth had been praying for the Lord to provide her with some sort of distraction from her problems? It seemed almost too good to be true! Turning toward Lillie, Beth felt like she was almost asking her daughter for permission. She didn't know if she wanted Lillie's response to be yes or no.

To her surprise, Lillie wore an enthusiastic smile on her face and was nodding vigorously. "Yes, Mom! Go for it!"

"I don't know," Beth mumbled. "I haven't been back to Rainbow Haven Beach since I left as a young adult. I put that place out of my mind when I chose to move to Ottawa and see what the world had to offer. It seems senseless to go back now…" Shaking her head, she added, "Besides, Kathy doesn't actually need my help. She is probably just hoping to give me a chance to get away for a little while."

"Mom!" Lillie reached out to touch Beth on the arm, her eyes wide but her expression soft. "Weren't we just talking about you finding somewhere to vacation for a while? How could there be any better an opportunity? You'd be crazy not to go!"

Nodding her head in acquiescence, Beth felt a surge of something akin to excitement whip through her body. It felt like the first sign of life that she had experienced since Ken got sick with cancer. But just as quickly as it had hit her, it passed. "What about you? Lillie, this is your Spring Break and you came to spend it with me…I can't leave you!"

Reaching out to tenderly take her mother's hands in her own, Lillie smiled. "I could use some time away, too, and I've always wanted to see where you grew up. If your friend will let me help, I'll go with you!"

Relief washed over Beth. Grabbing her daughter up in a hug, tears began to slip down her cheeks, and for the first time in years, they were actually tears of joy. Beth Campbell was finally going home.

SITTING IN THE DRIVER'S seat of the black compact car that they had rented from the airport, Lillie glanced at the GPS directions on her phone one more time. The last twenty-four hours had been a whirlwind of excitement, with Beth taking a week of leave from work at the magazine. They had purchased plane tickets that took them to Nova Scotia and were now traveling by rental car toward Rainbow Haven Beach.

Lowering the car window a little more, Lillie breathed in the fresh scent of the country air mingled with the ocean breeze. Lighthouses sprung up in their path sporadically, making her wish that she had time to stop and take pictures of every beautiful sight along their journey toward Kathy's house.

Glancing toward her mother, Lillie was relieved to see peace on Beth's face for the first time in a long time. Her mother was staring out the window, something almost like a smile playing on her lips.

"This place is beautiful." Lillie directed the car around a bend in the road. "Why didn't you ever bring me and Brian here to visit?"

Shrugging, Beth explained, "When I left Rainbow Haven, I felt like I was leaving it for good. I didn't have any plans to come back. And after my parents were both killed in a car wreck the fall that I was at university, it cut all ties with family here as well. Rainbow Haven was a place in the past for me, and the big city was the future. I was determined to make my mark in the world, and I thought that this place would only hinder me." Closing her eyes, she breathed in deeply and whispered, "But it certainly is good to be back."

Nodding, Lillie didn't have to verbalize her agreement. Even though she had never been to the area before, it felt more like home than anything else she had ever experienced. Her GPS alerted her that the destination was just ahead, and Lillie slowed the car to a crawl. The sight of a white clapboard cottage came into view, its image like something that might be pictured in an old Lucy Maude Montgomery book. As she pulled the car to a stop, Lillie was glad to get out and stretch her legs. She and Beth had hardly stepped out of the car when the front door of the house opened, and a pudgy short woman came rushing toward them.

"Beth! Beth!" the woman screeched animatedly, the loose gray bun on the back of her head bouncing up and down with her every step. Practically throwing herself into Beth's arms, she hugged the smaller woman against her before pulling away and saying, "It's so good to have you home!"

"It's good to be home!" Beth replied sincerely, the peace on her face now even more evident. Stepping back, she pointed toward Lillie as she explained, "Lillie, I'd like you to meet my childhood friend, Kathy. And Kathy, I don't know if you remember her, but this is my daughter, Lillie."

Before Lillie could say a word, Kathy had stepped forward to envelop her in a hug that equaled the one she had just given Beth. When Kathy pulled back, she had a wide smile on her face. "Welcome, Lillie! I am so excited to get to know you and to tell you stories about some of the antics that your mom and I got up to when we were younger."

Beth laughed with abandon and said, "Oh, you'd better not go there! We may just get in this car and drive back to the airport."

"Come on, get your bags and come inside!" Kathy urged. "Today we just spend the day visiting. Tomorrow, we look over the paint job."

Walking over to the car, they began to pull suitcases out of the trunk and then carried them to the house. Following behind her mother and Kathy, Lillie smiled softly to herself as she watched the two women walking side by side.

From the moment they arrived at Rainbow Haven Beach, Lillie had seen a tremendous and noticeable change in her mother. Watching Beth laughing now, it was hard to conceive that she was the same woman who had been standing over a grave in tearful, dismal silence only a day earlier.

Taking in a deep breath of the fresh air, Lillie's glance panned toward the beach that was only a few miles downhill from them. The waves that were rolling up on the shore seemed to call to her, and Lillie felt compelled to go down and dip her toes in the water. Forcing herself to ignore it and follow Beth into the house, Lillie promised herself that she would go spend some time at the water's edge before their vacation was over.

She decided that coming home to Rainbow Haven had been a good decision for Beth, and she could only hope that this short trip away from home would ultimately help both her and her mother. Perhaps this was the very spot she needed to be to get her mind off her own troubles, too, and refocus on what the best direction for her life should be.

Chapter Three

Stretching her arms over her head in the small twin-bed, Beth took in a deep breath of air and smiled contentedly. It didn't take more than a split second for her to remember where she was. As soon as she opened her eyes that morning, she had instantly recognized the fresh smell of the air and the velvety touch of value sheets on the mattress beneath her body. Pulling herself to her feet, she hurried to get dressed. For the first time since Ken was diagnosed with cancer, she found herself actually anticipating what the day might bring.

Once dressed, Beth made her way down the stairs and toward the kitchen. Glancing out the screen door to the back porch, she spied Kathy sitting at a picnic table, a cup of coffee in front of her and a book spread out on the tabletop her morning companions. The screen door creaked in protest as Beth opened it and stepped out onto the plank porch to make her way to Kathy's side.

"Good morning!" Kathy announced as she grinned up at her. "I thought I'd let you all sleep in this morning. No sense in starting out your time away from home by cracking the whip too hard."

Chuckling at her friend's statement, Beth took a seat across from Kathy. She declined the plate of pancakes that Kathy passed her direction with a polite shake of her head before looking out across the expanse of countryside, then closing her eyes and taking in another deep breath. The feeling had barely even finished its journey from her heart to her mind to take form when Beth heard herself whisper, "It's good to be back home."

Closing her book slowly, Kathy sat up straighter in her chair and reached for another pancake. Eyeing her friend as she took a bite, she said, "I think I heard you say the same thing yesterday. Pretty bold words for the girl who once told me she was going to leave Rainbow Haven and never come back."

Beth chuckled at the bittersweet words. Finally giving in to the sticky sweet smell of the maple syrup permeating the crisp morning air, she placed a pancake on her plate as she explained, "Well, I was young and naive at that point. I thought that the big city held all the answers for me. It was going to be my key to success and happiness."

"But it fell a little short of your expectations?"

Taking a bite of her pancake and reveling in its doughy sugariness, Beth exhaled a deep breath as she admitted, "It has had its benefits, but I didn't expect it would come with so many hardships and pain and at such a price." Beth swallowed past the lump in her throat. It hit her how true the admission was—so much sadness had come with her move. She had managed to have a good marriage and raise two children that she loved but being in a sea of people did little to comfort her when she was at her lowest. She had discovered that the fame and glory of her material success was superficial when it came to the rubber meeting the road.

The sound of the back door opening jolted both of them out of the quiet sad moment of reflection. Lillie made her way out onto the porch, rubbing her eyes and yawning as she ambled to the table.

"I don't think I've ever slept so peacefully in my life." Lillie took a sip of the bottled water that she had carried out with her. Leaning her head back against the chair, she smiled as she announced, "I just got to Rainbow Haven Beach, and yet it feels like I've already fallen in love. I think I could stay here for the rest of my life."

Beth understood her daughter's comment with her whole being. And, while she knew that Lillie would likely miss her boyfriend and university if she was away for more than a few days, Beth mirrored the sentiment.

Slapping her hands on the top of the table, Kathy declared, "Well, I didn't just invite you two here so that you could vacation. It's time for us to get to work!"

The women laughed together as they stood and headed out to the garage to gather their paint supplies. Beth doubted that working was going to cast even the slightest shadow on her time back at home; rather, it would keep her mind off everything that had been plaguing her, and for now, that was enough.

KATHY'S MOST RECENTLY purchased house was a small one-story country home several miles from the beachfront. As she explained on the short drive there, it had initially been inhabited by an elderly woman and her twelve cats. After she passed away, the house had been in such deplorable condition that her children sold it to Kathy for a steal, more anxious to simply have it off their hands than anything else.

"As you can see, it's not in bad shape now." Kathy set up some cans of paint in the large living room area. Pointing toward the walls, she elaborated, "The walls had to be repaired in a few places, but the flooring has been the main issue. All the carpeting had to be ripped up, and some of the hardwood actually had to be replaced. The bathroom was leaking, so it's still a work in progress."

Pouring some of the light blue paint into a tray, Beth listened to Kathy talk and marveled at the story. Kathy had managed to stay right there in their hometown, and while she may not have made herself famous on a national scale, she certainly was successful in her own way. Successful enough to not have to worry about money—and perhaps as successful as anyone needed to be.

"What happened with the cats?" Lillie stood with a roller in one hand, staring at Kathy in white-faced horror. "Her children took them in, right?"

Laughing, Kathy lowered her paintbrush into the paint and began to cut in the corners of the room. "No, no such luck. They were considered a part of the deal. I hate cats, so of course, I didn't keep them."

"Then where are they now?" Lillie pressed, distress at the plight of the poor abandoned kitties evident in her posture and expression.

Beth smiled at her concern. A staunch volunteer at a local animal shelter in Ottawa, it was no shock that Lillie would be worried about the cats' situation.

"Oh, I didn't hurt them!" Kathy assured her with a chuckle. "I just began to harass the women at the church until I finally found them all loving homes." Raising an eyebrow, she turned to give Lillie a sly look as she declared, "I'm very influential among the women at church. They know that if they don't go along with my agenda, they'll end up being nominated to provide meals for the upcoming luncheons or else sing a solo in the next cantata. Taking in a cat was a good deal, comparatively speaking!"

Beth laughed heartily and shook her head at her friend's cheeky comment. They worked side by side, and Beth felt herself relaxing as the room slowly transformed. The fresh coat of paint erased the old and run-down appearance, magically turning it into one of vibrance and full of youth.

As she worked, Beth wished there were some way that she could repaint the canvas of her own life with such a simple exercise. While she would not change a thing where her family was concerned, losing Ken had shown her just how vacant her existence truly was aside from them.

Finally starting to feel fatigued, she straightened and sucked in a deep breath. Looking toward her friend, she was surprised to see that Kathy was still plowing forward, working to run a long-handled roller along the one remaining wall. Lillie had paused to look at something on her phone but was still doing her part to keep up with the job.

Smiling at the image, Beth announced, "I'm going to run into the other room to get a drink. I'll be right back."

"Ahhh...running out on the job already." Kathy grinned, her arms never slowing down as she worked. "I should have known you'd be the first to give up."

Rolling her eyes with a smile, Beth made her way toward the kitchen, where her Thermos sat on the counter beside the sink. Glimpsing down at her hands and seeing paint splatters, Beth glanced toward the sink only to discover that the faucet had been removed.

Unwilling to risk covering her Thermos in blue paint, she muttered, "The bathroom has to be around here somewhere." Trailing through the house, she weaved her way past another bedroom and a small dining room. Rounding a bend in the hall, she spotted what she could only assume was the bathroom. Boldly stepping into the room, she was relieved to see that the sink appeared to be in working order.

Turning on the faucet, she began to scrub the paint off her hands. A glance into the mirror elicited a giggle at the sight of flecks of blue paint sprinkled throughout her shoulder-length brown hair. Her heart dropped to her toes in fright as she noticed something moving behind her in the shower. Spinning around on her heels without even drying her hands, Beth sent splashes of water in all directions as she screeched in shock. *What is a man doing crouching in Kathy's shower?! Does she know we have company?*

The man looked stunned at the unbridled scream, and he hurried to his feet, spinning around to face her fully. "Jeez, I am so sorry! I didn't mean to scare you." Waving the metal trowel that he held in his hand, he explained, "I'm here doing some tile work—" He stopped and peered at her with a frown. "Wait...Beth? Beth Barnett?"

Beth could hardly believe her own eyes. If she hadn't been so busy panicking at the sight of a stranger in the shower, she might have noticed sooner that the man looked familiar.

"Sean P...Pennington?" Beth found herself stumbling across the name. "Is that actually you?"

It had been almost forty years since she last saw him, and she would have happily gone another forty without seeing him. He still inspired the same uncomfortable riot of emotions he did in the days when they'd both been living here in Rainbow Haven Beach. Unwittingly letting her gaze roam across him from head to foot, she felt her face grow warm as she realized that he was doing the same to her.

He had certainly aged in the last thirty-eight-years. His face had thinned, and he had fine wrinkles around his eyes. His black hair was more silver now. Yet, despite the passage of time, he still had the same boyish charm that he had possessed when they were teenagers. Images of their last meeting flooded Beth's mind, and she had to swallow hard to keep herself in check. Shock, sadness, longing, and a little embarrassment washed over her just as they had back then.

"Yes, it's me." He finally managed an answer to her question. "At least, I think it's me. I'm surprised you still recognize me after all these years."

"What are you doing here?" Beth hoped her tone was even and didn't betray the emotions that she was battling.

Shrugging, Sean replied, "Seems I followed in my old man's footsteps after all. I'm in the remodeling business, and I've been helping Kathy get this place ready to go on the market. I'm down to the last little bit." His eyes narrowed as he studied Beth. "Are you here for long?"

Shaking her head, Beth subconsciously wiped her wet hands on the back of her jeans. "Just here visiting Kathy for a few days...Trying to help her get the paint job finished."

Nodding, Sean glanced back toward the shower. "Well, I'd better spread this grout before it starts to dry. It was good to see you, Beth. Maybe we can see each other again before you leave."

"It was a surprise to see you, too." She wanted nothing more than to race out of the bathroom and back toward the safety of the living room. She didn't say anything in reply to Sean's comment about meeting again. If Beth had her way, she would be avoiding him for the rest of her time at

Rainbow Haven Beach. Too much water had passed under that bridge to ever try to revisit it.

Chapter Four

Beth smiled from her comfy beach chair as she watched her daughter walking up and down the sandy shore, searching for seashells. It had been a long day of hard work, and Beth's arms were so sore she could hardly lift them. She was glad to see that Lillie had enough youthful vigor to make her way along the beach.

"You two really were a lot of help today." Kathy also watched Lillie's progress. "I appreciate it more than you know. If we keep up at this rate, we might have this house finished faster than I had expected."

Beth chuckled. "Come on, Kathy. That's silly, and you know it. We might have been help, but you could have found someone right here around Halifax that could have done just as much." Raising an eyebrow, Beth said, "I think that you just wanted to give me a little change in scenery."

Kathy shrugged innocently. "Was that such a bad idea?"

Watching Lillie bend over to pick something up off the sand, Beth shook her head slowly. "No. Not at all. We've only been here a little over a day, yet I can already see a 180-degree change in my spirits. It feels like I finally have a reason to live again. You, my old friend, have given me some hope in what was starting to feel like a dismal existence."

Turning to look at her, Kathy smiled and said, "Then I guess my mission is accomplished... Plus, I managed to get the house painted at the same time."

Chuckling to herself, Beth grew more somber as she remembered her encounter in the bathroom earlier that day. "I do wish that you'd mentioned that the work inside the house was being done while we're here."

"Work inside the house?" A gentle spring breeze danced across the beach, and Kathy reached up to hold onto her hat. "What do you mean?"

"Sean Pennington." Beth's face flushed. "I had no idea that I'd be seeing him."

Rolling her eyes and flipping a nonchalant hand, Kathy tsked, "Oh, Beth, surely you're not living in the past on that one, too, are you? Good grief, it's been almost forty years! I wasn't even thinking anything about it. Sean is just one of the best remodelers in our area, and I've hired him for several projects. If I can't do it myself, Sean usually can. I had expected him to be done with the job by the time that you arrived."

Beth regretted even bringing him up. Of course, she was making a mountain out of a molehill. Still, she was unable to curb her curiosity. "He's married now, isn't he?" She turned to watch Kathy, whose eyes were on the rolling waves.

Frowning slightly, Kathy replied, "Divorced. They finally broke up several years ago. Can't really say that anyone saw it come as a surprise. Sean's wife wasn't able to have children, and she had a much-requited interest in other men. I guess she finally found someone who she felt could offer her more than Sean."

Just as I did. The thought evoked physical pain as it crossed Beth's mind. She wished that the thoughts from so long ago that she had stuffed in the recesses of her mind, relegated to behind a "No Entry" sign, hadn't been unlocked with the key of her presence in Rainbow Haven Beach once again.

"Her name was Jennifer," Kathy informed her, almost as if it was her duty to fill Beth in on the entire story. "The girl was trouble from the time that they first started dating, but I guess no one could tell him. They broke up multiple times, but they always got back together. But this last time, she remarried, and she's been gone for almost ten years."

Despite the awkward memories she preferred to ignore, Beth's heart ached for her childhood friend. While she and Sean might have had their own rough history, he certainly didn't deserve such a sad ending to his romantic life. All things considered, Beth silently conceded to herself that her own heart-rending romance with Ken had a far better ending than what Sean had experienced with his wife.

Not willing to dwell on Sean any longer, Beth forced herself to change the subject and started talking about the houses that Kathy had been working on of late. Listening to her friend fill her in on all the details of her life, Beth leaned back in her chair and soaked in the warmth of the spring afternoon. She might not be staying at Rainbow Haven Beach for long, but Beth was determined that she was going to savor every minute that she could at her old stomping grounds.

LILLIE REACHED UP TO push a strand of blonde hair out of her face which the ocean breeze had gently displaced as she walked along the beach. Her eyes remained fixed on the ground, looking for any unusual or particularly striking shell that might catch her attention. While her days at Rainbow Haven Beach might be numbered, already she knew that it was going to remain a memorable visit for years to come, and she wanted to take home some pieces of it when they returned to the city. It would give her a semblance of peace whenever she looked at them and was reminded of a time when things had seemed happy.

Twisting her left hand toward her to view her iPhone, she spotted the text waiting for a reply, and her heart sank. *Lukas.* He wanted her to call him. Well, *want* was an understatement. He'd demanded it. She'd been ignoring his phone calls all day, trying to pretend that she wasn't haunted by every buzz and notification.

Sucking in a fortifying breath of air, Lillie decided that it was best to get it over with. Lifting the phone and pushing the call button, she swallowed thickly. Holding it up to her ear, she waited for her boyfriend to answer.

His anger was impossible to miss when he picked up. "It's about time!"

His tone alone tempted Lillie to hang up and end their communication immediately, but she forced herself to endure his attitude. She'd been ignoring him, after all. No one liked being ignored—Lukas less than most—and she'd been fully cognizant of this whilst doing it. He had every right to be upset.

"What's going on?" Lukas pressed. "You run off to visit your mom, supposedly, and now you don't even want to return my calls."

"I'm sorry, Lukas." Lillie heaved a sigh as she bent over to pick a green spiraled seashell up off the beach. "It's been a whirlwind the last few hours. My mom got a letter from a friend asking her to visit her hometown, so we took a little detour from our original plans and ended up leaving Ottawa for a while."

She tensed the moment the words were out, heart hammering as she waited for the usual outburst that came whenever she failed to tell Lukas what she was doing and where she was going.

As anticipated, Lukas's annoyance flared to outright anger, and his voice rose in both volume and timbre. "What is that supposed to mean? You left Ottawa? Then, where are you?"

Trying to appear nonchalant about the entire matter, Lillie broke the news. "Well, we ended up coming to a little place called Rainbow Haven Beach... It's in Nova Scotia."

The dead silence on the other end of the phone made Lillie wonder if she had somehow lost phone service. Truth be told, she secretly hoped this was the case and there would be no further reply. Tentatively, she pressed, "Lukas?"

To her disappointment, he muttered a curse and repeated, "Nova Scotia." Cursing again, he snapped, "We're not going to talk about this now, Lillie Campbell, but you can bet that we're going to have plenty to discuss once you get back home."

Before she could even formulate an answer, a click on the other end of the line signaled that Lukas had hung up on her and that as far as he was concerned, the conversation was over. Hot tears filled Lillie's eyes as she considered all that had just transpired between them. She knew that leaving town without informing her boyfriend was a bad idea, but she had seen no other option. She wished that Lukas was someone sympathetic and compassionate who would be a sounding board for her concerns about her mother and maybe even help her brainstorm ways to make Beth's life better. But that was far from the case.

Lukas was selfish and self-absorbed, through and through. If Lillie had even mentioned the idea of going with her mother to Rainbow Haven Beach, he would have nixed the idea completely, informing her that under no uncertain terms was she allowed to travel out of the city. By omitting to inform him, she had at least been able to avoid going directly against his will. A sudden surge of anger swelled through her at herself for even caring. *I'm not a child, and he isn't my parent!* He had no right to refuse her going on a trip with her mother. She reached up shakily to wipe an errant tear. She was near breaking point. Instead of treating her like the woman he loved, Lukas was someone that was determined to control and manipulate her at all costs.

Over the last few years, Lillie had kept trying to assure herself that things with Lukas would get better with time. How could they not? He had swept her off her feet the first day of university, winning her over with his charismatic charm and contagious smile. Yet, it seemed that the longer they were together, the more domineering and manipulative he became. "It will get better once we've graduated," Lillie muttered to herself. "We've just both been under a lot of stress. He'll change once he's not worried about tests and grades." Even as she tried to appease herself with the words, they echoed hollowly. People could change under stress, but they didn't change this much, did they? Had he been like this all along? Perhaps she simply hadn't noticed.

Turning to look back toward her mother and Kathy, who were still sitting together in their chairs, Lillie realized just how far she had walked on her meander down the beach. The sun was starting to set, casting beautiful shadowy patterns on the water. Deep in her heart, Lillie wished that there was some way that she could simply stay at Rainbow Haven Beach and never have to go back to Ottawa at all. It would be a relief and a blessing to walk away from the challenges of her life with Lukas and start over fresh, free of him and his aggressive, controlling manner and degrading attitude.

Perhaps this vacation had been a bad idea. Rather than provide her with the break she had wanted, it had only glaringly highlighted the new beginning Lillie so desperately needed. Would she be able to live her old life when she had to return to Ottawa, or would this break make it unbearable? A sinking feeling confirmed her suspicion that it would be the latter.

LETTING OUT AN IMPRESSED whistle, Kathy stepped back and cocked her head to one side. "Well, I do have to declare, we have made this old place look good!"

Beth, taking a step back, too, let her eyes travel over the now soft-purple wall in the bedroom. Over the last few days, each room in the house had been carefully rolled and brushed, providing new life to the otherwise dull areas.

"What do you think?" Kathy asked as she spread out her arms. "Ready for viewing by the buyers, wouldn't you say?"

Beth nodded enthusiastically and smiled, "Yes, I would say so." Though she was optimistic and tried to sound as much, it was impossible to ignore the ball of emotions that was forming in her throat.

This had been one of the best weeks of Beth's adult life. Away from the relentless pace of the city and the heartache of her husband's memory, Beth had been able to simply enjoy herself. She had been able to laugh with her old friend, reconnect with her daughter, and embrace the simpler side of life.

And what awaited her now? A trip back to the city.

Beth's heart sank at the thought of going back to her lonely townhouse with its huge rooms that were only full of material things and painful memories. She could hardly stand the idea of getting up and going to work each day only to come home to go to sleep by herself each night. She had reached the pinnacle of what she had considered success as a young woman, yet she had discovered that it was far from what she actually needed deep within her soul.

"I'm going to go get my drink." Lillie headed into the other room, leaving Kathy and Beth alone.

Kathy was cleaning up the last of their paint mess, folding up drop sheets and putting lids on paint cans. Standing up straight, she looked toward Beth and said, "You don't seem nearly as happy to be finished with the job as you were when we were teenagers painting my bedroom."

Laughing softly, Beth looked down at her hands and began to pick at some paint that was stuck to her palm. Shaking her head slowly, she could only hope that she didn't sound as discouraged as she felt when she said, "I guess I'm just dreading that long flight back home! I know it has to happen, but being back at Rainbow Haven has been a relief. It's been good to be out of the rat race for a while. One forgets how peaceful life is here."

Standing up straighter, Kathy shook her head. "Then stay for a bit longer. You don't have to leave right away. There's no need to, so stay until you're ready to leave."

The idea was so appealing that Beth almost said yes on the spot, but she forced herself to be mature about it. "No, I think I need to get back home. I'm keeping Lillie away from her boyfriend, and she has classes starting again soon."

How could she explain that if she was to stay at Rainbow Haven until she was ready to leave, she might never go at all?

Biting down on her lip, Kathy seemed to be considering everything that she was hearing. Finally, she gave a nod. "Well, if you need to go, then so be it. But at least stay until after church on Sunday! It would be so nice to have you back at the church for services. We can sit together like we did when we were little girls...minus some of our old gossiping, of course." She reached out to elbow Beth good-naturedly and added, "But maybe just a bit of it."

Smiling slightly as she considered the offer, Beth finally agreed. "All right. We can stay until Sunday. But after church, we will need to see about getting back to Ottawa."

She was glad that she had at least agreed to stay for church. Deep in her heart, Beth was in no hurry to leave Rainbow Haven Beach, and each day that she got to stay felt like a blessing.

Chapter Five

From her seat in the hardwood pew in the small church, Beth's eyes traveled toward the beautiful stained-glass windows. How often she had sat in that very pew as a little girl and looked toward the windows, silently marveling that they were like a window into heaven. In the background, she could hear Kathy's voice booming out the words to a familiar hymn, yet Beth didn't follow suit. Instead, she allowed her mind to run free.

She silently considered just how long it had been since she sat in a pew at church. Of course, Beth had always been a believer in the Lord and had always considered herself a Christian, but as life became hectic, He was pushed to the backburner. Life became less about following a Higher Power and more about achieving her own success. The revelation of her misplaced priorities left her with a deep sense of shame. Didn't the Bible say that you reap what you sow? Surely, Beth was now reaping the harvest that she had been planting her entire adult life. With a life that had been focused mainly on money, she was finding herself left with nothing but her money and the stark reality of how cold and empty a friendship it provided.

As the hymn came to a close, the minister stood up to announce, "Let us pray."

Bowing her head, Beth tried to listen to his words, but it felt like she couldn't even comprehend them. Closing her eyes, she found herself whispering words of her own, talking to the Lord about the struggles that she was facing in her own heart.

Is it too late for me, Lord? she asked silently. *Have I done too much to ever make things right? I feel like I'm all alone in the world. I have spent my life chasing fame and fortune, only to find my place all alone with my husband dead and my children grown up. I'm tired of trying to live for money. I want to live for something greater. Is there any chance that You have a different plan for me in mind?*

The words seemed so paltry. It seemed presumptuous to think that the Creator might still have a plan for her after she'd strayed so far from Him over the years. But just as she was thinking about how futile it was for her to have asked, she felt a whispered answer wash over her.

Stay.

It felt like every fiber of her being was overwhelmed by the prompting. Perhaps she had wasted the last fifty-eight years of her life trying to be successful in the eyes of the world, but that didn't mean that it was too late for her to do a turnaround now.

Perhaps the Lord still had a plan for her life. The plan might require giving up everything that she had once held dear and used as an anchor in life's storms, but it might be just what she needed to finally embrace the life she was meant to live.

Tears began to cloud Beth's vision, and she reached up to wipe at her mascara. Her heart thumped with a surge of happiness, excitement, and expectation that she hadn't experienced in years. Maybe her life wasn't over after all. Maybe it was just beginning.

"IT SURE WAS NICE TO have my best friend back in church with me." Kathy directed her car down the road that led back toward her cottage home. "Even if we didn't gossip quite as much as we did when we were younger," she added impishly.

From her spot in the passenger seat, Beth sensed Kathy giving her a sideways glance. While Kathy was chattering away like a schoolgirl, it was easy for Beth to discern that her friend was worried. Beth was so consumed by her thoughts that she had hardly spoken a word since they left the service, and she was sure that her companions were noticing.

"What did you think of the sermon?" Kathy pressed, turning to look directly at Beth.

Shrugging, Beth replied, "It was nice. Very nice." Trying to think of something else to add, she said, "He seems like a good speaker."

Kathy diverted her attention toward the back of the car where Lillie was sitting. "What about you?"

"I really liked it." Lillie spoke up with a bit more enthusiasm. "I hate to admit it, but I haven't gone to church much since I started university. Your church is really nice. It feels very welcoming and friendly, and the minister talked to us like we were friends."

Beth's nerves were in such a jumble that she could hardly hear what they were saying. In her suitcase inside Kathy's house, she had plane tickets back to Ottawa on the flight scheduled to leave that afternoon. Now, she was rethinking everything about her plans to leave.

Biting her lower lip, she wondered what Kathy would think when she declared that she planned to stay. Even more importantly, she wondered how Lillie would take the news. Surely, her daughter would think that she had lost her mind.

Pulling her car to a stop in front of her home, Kathy announced, "Well, I guess we better get you all inside. I know you've got a lot of packing to do, so I'm going to fix us a quick bite for lunch."

Stepping out of the car into the bright sunshine of the early afternoon, Beth's heart squeezed up into her throat.

"I'm about packed already." Lillie opened her own door and stepped out. She stopped when she saw the look on Beth's face and asked, "Do you need some help, Mom? Do you have much left to pack?"

Determined to make her announcement as quickly as possible, Beth shook her head slowly. Turning around so that she could look directly at her daughter and friend, her voice trembled as she said, "I've decided not to go."

The expressions on both women's faces were more shocked than Beth could have even imagined possible. If she weren't so nervous herself, she would've laughed to see her daughter with her mouth hanging open and Kathy's eyes as large as saucers.

"You what?" Lillie asked after a moment.

Looking toward the beach in the distance, Beth explained. "I think I've had enough of city life. Ottawa has nothing left for me now. My husband is gone, and my kids are adults, forging their own paths in life...All I do there is live to work and visit the cemetery. And I'm tired of just living to try to make money." Suddenly concerned about what Kathy might be thinking, she hurried to add, "I'll get a motel room until I find a place to live. I'm going to see what Rainbow Haven Beach has to offer now that I'm grown up and have my priorities reset."

"You will do no such thing!" Kathy's vehement outburst took Beth by surprise. With several long steps, she reached out to put an arm around Beth's shoulder and hurried to explain. "There will be no rented rooms as long as I'm still alive. You are going to stay here with me."

The suggestion seemed almost too good to be true. Tears spilled over and started to stream down Beth's cheeks, and she reached up to wipe them away as she asked, "Are you sure?"

Nodding, Kathy dabbed at her own eyes. "I've never been surer of anything in my life! This is like a dream come true." Reaching out to wrap her plump arms around her old friend, she confessed, "I've been hoping you would come home ever since you left!"

When Kathy let go of her, Beth stepped back so that she could survey Lillie. Her daughter was still standing beside the car with a stunned expression.

"Lillie?" Beth could only hope that her daughter would be understanding of her decision. "Are you going to be okay with this? I know it's abrupt, and it's a wild decision from your usually sane mother..."

"It's the best choice you've made in years." Lillie moved away from the car and made her way to her mother's side. "I've watched you working your rear off for as long as I can remember, and I've never seen you as happy as you've been while you were here at Rainbow Haven Beach." Reaching out and taking her mother's hands in her own, she added, "I think it's high time that you look forward to doing something that you want to do. Something that gives value and meaning to your life."

Although relieved to have the support of her friend and daughter, Beth found herself overwhelmed with fears as reality hit her full force. Somehow, being distracted by concerns about what they would think had delayed her thoughts about the minutiae of her move.

"W...what about my job?" Beth breathed, suddenly thinking of a thousand different loose ends. "And the house in the city? What about your father's company? And where am I going to find a house here?"

Giving her mother's hands an encouraging squeeze, Lillie smiled softly as she said, "Don't worry about it at all, Mom. I've actually been thinking about taking some time off from school so that I can stay with you. I've had too much on my own mind with missing Dad. I am going to see about transferring my classes online so that I can help you make this move."

While Beth didn't want to see her daughter give up her own plans, the offer of help felt like an answer to prayer. She pulled her daughter closer, embracing her while Kathy threw her arms exuberantly around both of them. Beth breathed a silent prayer of thanks as she considered her new direction in life. She didn't know what to expect now that she was moving back to Rainbow Haven Beach, but she was finally excited about the future and looking forward to whatever might unfold. It felt as if life had a purpose again, and she couldn't wait to see what tomorrow would bring.

DID YOU ENJOY YOUR trip to Rainbow Haven Beach? Find out more of what happens to Beth, Lillie, and Kathy as you follow them on their journeys of self-discovery.

Finding Hope (Rainbow Haven Beach Book 1)
After the death of her husband, Beth Campbell decides it's time for a fresh start. When she returns to her hometown in Nova Scotia, she discovers a beautiful old abandoned home by the seaside and imagines it as the perfect spot for her to run a bed and breakfast and finally have the chance to write a novel. But when she discovers that the house belongs to Sean Pennington, a man with whom she has a painful history, she begins to doubt her dream.

With the encouragement of her friends and newfound faith, Beth takes a chance on the dilapidated home and hires Sean as a skilled carpenter to help her restore it. As they work together to bring the old house back to life, Beth and Sean's shared history resurfaces, forcing them to confront unresolved feelings and past mistakes. Will they be able to forgive each other and move on, or will their complicated history keep them apart?

Finding Peace (Rainbow Haven Beach Book 2)
Finding Love (Rainbow Haven Beach Book 3)
Finding Home (Rainbow Haven Beach Book 4)
Finding Joy (Rainbow Haven Beach Book 5)
Finding Faith (Rainbow Haven Beach Book 6)

Thank you, readers!

THANK YOU FOR READING this book. It is important to me to share my stories with you and that you enjoy them. May I ask a favor of you? If you enjoyed this book, would you please take a moment to leave a review? Thank you for your support!

Also, each week, I send my readers updates about my life as well as information about my new releases, freebies, promos, and book recommendations. If you're interested in receiving my weekly newsletter, please go to newsletter.sylviaprice.com[1], and it will ask you for your email. As a thank-you, you will receive several FREE exclusive short stories that aren't available for purchase!

Blessings,

Sylvia

---

1.   http://newsletter.sylviaprice.com

Other Books by Sylvia Price

Songbird Cottage Beginnings (Pleasant Bay Prequel)
SET ON CANADA'S PICTURESQUE Cape Breton Island, this book is perfect for those who enjoy new beginnings and countryside landscapes.

Sam MacAuley and his wife Annalize are total opposites. When Sam wants to leave city life in Halifax to get a plot of land on Cape Breton Island, where he grew up, his wife wants nothing to do with his plans and opts to move herself and their three boys back to her home country of South Africa.

As Sam settles into a new life on his own, his friend Lachlan encourages him to get back into the dating scene. Although he meets plenty of women, he longs to find the one with whom he wants to share the rest of his life. Will Sam ever meet "the one"?

Get to know Sam and discover the origins of the Songbird Cottage. This is the prequel to the rest of the Pleasant Bay series.

The Crystal Crescent Inn Boxed Set (Sambro Lighthouse Complete Series Collection)

SYLVIA PRICE'S SAMBRO Lighthouse Series, set on Canada's picturesque Crystal Crescent Beach, is a feel-good read perfect for fans of second chances with a bit of history and mystery all rolled into one. Enjoy all five sweet romance books in one collection for the first time!

Liz Beckett is grief-stricken when her beloved husband of thirty-five years dies after a long battle with cancer. Her daughter and best friend insist she needs a project to keep her occupied. Liz decides to share the beauty of Crystal Crescent Beach with those who visit the beautiful east coast of Nova Scotia and prepares to embark on the adventure of her life. She moves into the converted art studio at the bottom of her garden and turns the old family home into The Crystal Crescent Inn.

One of her first visitors is famous archeologist, Merc MacGill, and he's not there to admire the view. The handsome bachelor believes there's an undiscovered eighteenth-century farmstead hidden inside the creeks and coves of Crystal Crescent, and Liz wants to help him find it.

But it's not all smooth sailing at the inn that overlooks the historic Sambro Lighthouse. No one has realized it yet, but the lives of everyone in Liz's family are intertwined with those first settlers who landed in Nova Scotia over two hundred and fifty years ago. Will they be able to unravel the mystery? Will the lives of Liz's two children be changed forever if they discover the link between the lighthouse and their old home?

Take a trip to Crystal Crescent Beach and join Liz, her family, and guests as they navigate the storms and calm waters of life and love under the watchful eye of the lighthouse and its secret.

Sarah (The Amish of Morrissey County Prequel)
WELCOME TO MORRISSEY County! This fictional region in Pennsylvania Amish country is home to several generations of strong-willed Amish women who know what they want in life, even if others disagree. Join these women on their search for love and acceptance.

Morrissey County, 1979

Sarah Kauffman has always abided by the *Ordnung*, and not only because her father happens to be the town's bishop and would, she feels, disown her if she didn't. But when her mother passes away, she longs to escape the clutches of her father and run away to the *Englisch* world. When her father wants her to marry someone she doesn't love, Sarah becomes even more desperate to leave.

Jacob Renno, on the other hand, is happy with life on his farm. It keeps him so busy that the older bachelor has no time for love, but on lonely nights, he finds himself longing for a companion.

When Sarah and Jacob meet, there's an instant connection, but things get complicated. Jacob offers to help Sarah with her dilemma, but Bishop Kaufmann insists that she obey his wishes. Will Sarah run off to join the *Englisch*, or will the handsome farmer give her pause? Will her father disown her or give her his blessing? Find out in this sweet Amish romance as you become immersed in the lives of these Morrissey County residents.

Sarah is the prequel to the Amish of Morrissey County series. Each book is a stand-alone read, but to make the most of the series, you should consider reading them in order.

The Origins of Cardinal Hill (The Amish of Cardinal Hill Prequel)
Two girls with a legacy to carry on. A third choosing to forge her own path.

WELCOME TO CARDINAL Hill, Indiana! This quaint fictional town is home to Faith Hochstetler, Leah Bontrager, Iris Mast, their families, and their trades. Faith, Leah, and Iris are united in their shared passion for turning their hobbies within nature into profitable businesses...and finding love! Find out how it all begins in this short, free prequel!

Other books in this series:

- *The Beekeeper's Calendar*: Faith's Story
- *The Soapmaker's Recipe*: Leah's Story
- *The Herbalist's Remedy*: Iris's Story

The Origins of Cardinal Hill is the prequel to the Amish of Cardinal Hill series. Each book is a stand-alone read, but to make the most of the series, you should consider reading them in order.

A Promised Tomorrow (The Yoder Family Saga Prequel)
THE YODER FAMILY SAGA follows widow Miriam Yoder and her four unmarried daughters, Megan, Rebecca, Josephine, and Lillian, as they discover God's plans for them and the hope He provides for a happy tomorrow.

The Yoder women struggle to survive after Jeremiah Yoder succumbs to a battle with cancer. The family risks losing their farm and their livelihood. They are desperate to find a way to keep going. Will Miriam and her daughters be able to work together to keep their family afloat? Will God pull through for them and provide for them in their time of need?

A Promised Tomorrow is the prequel to the Yoder Family Saga. Join the Yoder women through their journey of loss and hope for a better future. Each book is a stand-alone read, but to make the most of the series, you should consider reading them in order. Start reading this sweet Amish romance today that will take you on a rollercoaster of emotions as you're welcomed into the life of the Yoder family.

Jonah's Redemption: Book 1

JONAH HAS LOST HIS community, and he's struggling to get by in the English world. He yearns for his Amish roots, but his past mistakes keep him from returning home.

Mary Lou is recovering from a medical scare. Her journey has impressed upon her how precious life is, so she decides to go on *rumspringa* to see the world.

While in the city, Mary Lou meets Jonah. Unable to understand his foul attitude, especially towards her, she makes every effort to share her faith with him. As she helps him heal from his past, an attraction develops.

Will Jonah's heart soften towards Mary Lou? What will God do with these two broken people?

The Christmas Cards: An Amish Holiday Romance

LUCY YODER IS A YOUNG Amish widow who recently lost the love of her life, Albrecht. As Christmas approaches, she dreads what was once her favorite holiday, knowing that this Christmas was supposed to be the first one she and Albrecht shared together. Then, one December morning, Lucy discovers a Christmas card from an anonymous sender on her doorstep. Lucy receives more cards, all personal, all tender, all comforting. Who in the shadows is thinking of her at Christmas?

Andy Peachey was born with a rare genetic disorder. Coming to grips with his predicament makes him feel a profound connection to Lucy Yoder. Seeking meaning in life, he uses his talents to give Christmas cheer. Will Andy's efforts touch Lucy's heart and allow her to smile again? Or will Lucy, herself, get in his way?

The Christmas Cards is a story of loss and love and the ability to find yourself again in someone else.

About the Author

SYLVIA PRICE IS AN author of Amish and contemporary romance and women's fiction. She especially loves writing uplifting stories about second chances!

Sylvia was inspired to write about the Amish as a result of the enduring legacy of Mennonite missionaries in her life. While living with them for three weeks, they got her a library card and encouraged her to start reading to cope with the loss of television and radio, Sylvia developed a newfound appreciation for books.

Although raised in the cosmopolitan city of Montréal, Sylvia spent her adolescent and young adult years in Nova Scotia, and the beautiful countryside landscapes and ocean views serve as the backdrop to her contemporary novels.

After meeting and falling in love with an American while living abroad, Sylvia now resides in the US. She spends her days writing, hoping to inspire the next generation to read more stories. When she's not writing, Sylvia stays busy making sure her three young children are alive and well-fed.

SUBSCRIBE   TO   SYLVIA'S   newsletter   at
http://newsletter.sylviaprice.com[1] to stay in the loop about new releases,
freebies, promos, and more. As a thank-you, you will receive a FREE
exclusive short story that isn't available for purchase.

Follow   Sylvia   on   Facebook   at   http://facebook.com/
sylviapriceauthor for updates.

Join   Sylvia's   Advanced   Reader   Copies   (ARC)   team   at
http://arcteam.sylviaprice.com[2] to get her books for free before they are
released in exchange for honest reviews.

---

1. http://newsletter.sylviaprice.com/

2.   http://arcteam.sylviaprice.com/